·CLASSICS·
Illustrated®

Rudyard Kipling
THE JUNGLE BOOK

essay by
Gregory Feeley

ACCLAIM BOOKS
STUDY GUIDE

The Jungle Book

art by Alex Blum
cover by Alex Maleev

For Classics Illustrated Study Guides
computer recoloring by VanHook Studios
editor: Madeleine Robins
assistant editor: Gregg Sanderson
design: Scott Friedlander

Classics Illustrated: The Jungle Book © Twin Circle Publishing Co.,
a division of Frawley Enterprises; licensed to First Classics, Inc.
All new material and compilation © 1997 by Acclaim Books, Inc.

Dale-Chall R.L.: 7.25

ISBN 1-57840-064-3

Acclaim Books, New York, NY
Printed in the United States

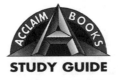

STUDY GUIDE

STRIPED CATTLE-KILLER! THE WOLVES ARE A FREE PEOPLE...WE TAKE NO ORDERS BUT FROM THE HEAD OF THE PACK. THE CUB IS OURS!

WHAT TALK IS THIS? IT IS I, SHERE KAHN, WHO SPEAKS!

AND IT IS I, RAKSHA, THE DEMON, WHO ANSWERS! THE MAN-CUB IS MINE. HE SHALL RUN WITH THE PACK AND HUNT WITH THE PACK AND IN THE END, O FROG-EATER, FISH-KILLER, GREAT HUNTER OF LITTLE NAKED CUBS, HE SHALL HUNT YOU! GO!

EACH DOG BARKS IN HIS OWN BACKYARD. WE SHALL SEE WHAT THE PACK SAYS ABOUT THIS ADOPTING OF MAN-CUBS.

THE CUB MUST BE SHOWN TO THE PACK. WILL YOU KEEP HIM?

ASSUREDLY! MOWGLI, THE FROG, WILL I CALL YOU! YES, ONE DAY YOU SHALL HUNT SHERE KAHN AS HE HAS HUNTED YOU!

THE LAW OF THE JUNGLE SAYS VERY CLEARLY THAT WHEN THE CUBS ARE OLD ENOUGH TO STAND, THEY SHALL BE BROUGHT TO THE PACK COUNCIL SO THAT THE OTHER WOLVES WILL KNOW THEM AND LEAVE THEM UNHARMED...YES MOWGLI MUST BE SHOWN TO THE PACK...AND ONE NIGHT, A FEW MONTHS LATER, IN THE LIGHT OF THE FULL MOON...

...AND SO MOWGLI, THE FROG, WAS ACCEPTED INTO THE WOLF PACK...

IT WAS WELL DONE. MEN AND THEIR CUBS ARE VERY WISE. THIS MAN-CUB MAY BE A HELP IN TIME.

AY, ROAR WELL, SHERE KAHN, FOR THE TIME WILL COME WHEN THIS LITTLE CUB WILL MAKE YOU ROAR ANOTHER TUNE!

FOR TEN HAPPY YEARS, MOWGLI GREW AND LEARNED THE MEANINGS OF THINGS IN THE JUNGLE, EVERY RUSTLE IN THE GRASS, EVERY SCRATCH OF THE BAT'S CLAWS, EVERY SPLASH OF THE FISH JUMPING IN THE POOL.

BAGHEERA TAUGHT HIM TO CLIMB...

...AND HE PICKED THE THORNS OUT OF THE PADS OF HIS BROTHER WOLVES' PAWS...

...AND HE TOOK HIS PLACE AT THE COUNCIL...

...AND ALSO, HE DISCOVERED A STRANGE POWER WITHIN HIMSELF.

AKELA WAS PLACED BY THE SIDE OF THE COUNCIL ROCK...A SIGN THAT THE LEADERSHIP OF THE PACK WAS OPEN...

BEING ASKED TO SPEAK... AND SINCE THE LEADERSHIP OF THE PACK IS OPEN...I WISH TO SAY...

FREE PEOPLE! DOES SHERE KAHN LEAD THE PACK? WHAT HAS A TIGER TO DO WITH OUR LEADERSHIP?

ARE WE ALL JACKALS TO FAWN ON THIS CATTLE-BUTCHER? THE LEADERSHIP OF THE PACK IS WITH THE PACK ALONE!

SILENCE, MAN-CUB!

SHERE KAHN HAS KEPT THE LAW!

LET THE DEAD WOLF SPEAK!

WHEN THE LEADER OF THE PACK MISSED HIS KILL, HE WAS CALLED THE "DEAD WOLF" AS LONG AS HE LIVED...

FREE PEOPLE! AND YOU, TOO, JACKALS OF SHERE KAHN! FOR MANY YEARS I HAVE LED YOU... NOW, I HAVE MISSED MY KILL. YOUR RIGHT IS TO KILL ME HERE ON THE COUNCIL ROCK....IT IS MY RIGHT, BY THE LAW OF THE JUNGLE, THAT YOU COME ONE BY ONE! WHO COMES TO MAKE AN END OF THE LONE WOLF?

...BUT NO ONE DARED...

IF YOU WILL LET THE MAN-CUB GO, I WILL DIE WITHOUT FIGHTING! THIS WILL SAVE THE PACK AT LEAST THREE LIVES!

BUT AKELA'S PLEA WAS TO NO AVAIL. THE PACK CLOSED IN FOR THE KILL...

NOW THE BUSINESS IS IN YOUR HANDS, LITTLE FROG! WE CAN DO NO MORE THAN FIGHT!

LISTEN, YOU! THERE IS NO NEED FOR THIS DOG'S JABBER!

I WOULD HAVE BEEN YOUR BROTHER TILL MY LIFE'S END, BUT SINCE YOU WOULD NOT HAVE IT SO, I NO LONGER CALL YOU BROTHERS, BUT DOGS! WHAT YOU WILL OR WILL NOT DO IS FOR ME...A MAN...TO SAY! LOOK!

I, THE MAN, HAVE BROUGHT YOU THE RED FLOWER WHICH YOU DOGS FEAR SO MUCH!

YOU ARE MASTER NOW, O MOWGLI! SAVE AKELA... HE WAS EVER YOUR FRIEND!

...MOWGLI WAS SWIMMING IN A JUNGLE POOL WITH HIS FRIEND, KAA, THE GIANT ROCK PYTHON.

WHAT MORE CAN I WISH? I HAVE THE JUNGLE. ALL THAT ARE OF THE JUNGLE ARE MY FRIENDS. I HAVE THE POOLS, THE NOOKS, THE TREES... AND YOU, FRIEND FLATHEAD!

I WILL TELL YOU. NOW, THE COBRA SAID...

WHAT COBRA? HAVE YOU MANY DEALINGS WITH THE POISON PEOPLE? I GIVE THEM THEIR OWN PATH. THEY CARRY DEATH IN THEIR FORETOOTH. WHAT COBRA?... AND WHAT DID HE SAY?

THREE OR FOUR MOONS AGO, I HUNTED IN A FAR-OFF PLACE. A KING COBRA THERE SHOWED ME MANY THINGS I HAD NEVER SEEN BEFORE. HE SAID THAT MAN WOULD GIVE THE BREATH UNDER HIS RIBS FOR THE SIGHT OF THESE THINGS.

I WOULD LIKE TO LOOK AT THIS NEW GAME, KAA. LET US GO!

IT IS NOT GAME... IT IS... IT IS... I KNOW NOT WHAT IT IS...

WE WILL GO THERE! I HAVE NEVER SEEN A KING COBRA... AND I WISH TO SEE THE OTHER THINGS. DID HE KILL THEM?

THEY ARE ALL DEAD. HE SAYS HE IS KEEPER OF THEM ALL.

LET US GO AS SOON AS I HAVE DRIED MY-SELF IN THIS GRASS.

AND SO MOWGLI AND KAA SET OUT FOR THE COBRA AND THE THINGS HE GUARDED.

THIS WAY, LITTLE BROTHER, THIS WAY!

NIGHT FELL. STILL KAA SLID AHEAD UNTIL THE JUNGLE THINNED AND...

WHAT IS THIS PLACE KAA? I HAVE NEVER SEEN ANYTHING LIKE IT.

THE BANDER-LOG' CALL IT THEIR HOLY CITY. BUT TO THE JUNGLE, IT IS KNOWN AS THE COLD LAIRS. MEN LIVED HERE LONG AGO. COME! THIS WAY LIES THE WHITE HOOD AND HIS PILE₃

'MONKEYS

SOMETHING TELLS ME THIS TOOTH' WILL SEE WORK TONIGHT... LEAD ON, KAA!

'DAGGER

KAA SLIPPED OVER A PILE OF RUBBISH AND SUDDENLY DARTED UNDERGROUND THROUGH AN OLD DOOR...

FEARING UNFRIENDLY SNAKES, MONGLI GAVE THE SNAKE-CALL WHICH BALOO, THE BEAR, HAD TAUGHT HIM...

HSSS...SS...SSH. WE BE OF ONE BLOOD, YOU AND I!

COME, LITTLE BROTHER! IN HERE...FOLLOW QUICKLY OR YOU WILL LOSE ME!

TENSE, ON HIS GUARD, MONGLI FOLLOWED.

BY THE BULL THAT BOUGHT ME! A SAFE LAIR INDEED! BUT I SEE NOTHING!

AM I NOTHING?

AS MONGLI'S EYES BECAME ACCUSTOMED TO THE DARKNESS, HE SAW...

GOOD HUNTING, O FATHER OF THE COBRAS!

WHAT DO YOU THINK OF OUR CITY, O MANLING... AND OF THE HUNDRED ELEPHANTS AND THE TWENTY THOUSAND HORSES...THE CITY OF THE KING OF TWENTY KINGS?

THERE IS NO CITY ABOVE US...ONLY THE JUNGLE. AND...WHAT IS A KING?

I TOLD YOU FOUR MONTHS AGO, THAT YOUR CITY WAS NO MORE.

THE GREAT CITY CAN NEVER PASS! IT WAS MADE IN THE DAYS OF BAPPA RAWAL AND SHALL ENDURE WHEN MY SON'S SONS ARE AS WHITE AS I. WHOSE CATTLE ARE YOU THAT YOU DO NOT KNOW THIS?

HIS GREAT CITY IS NOTHING MORE THAN A LOST TRAIL, KAA. I DO NOT UNDERSTAND HIS TALK.

NOR I. HE IS VERY OLD AND SPEAKS OF THINGS BEFORE MY TIME.

THE OBJECT THAT ATTRACTED MOWGLI WAS A BEAUTIFULLY JEWELED ANKUS...

IS IT NOT WORTH DYING TO BEHOLD? HAVE I NOT DONE YOU A GREAT FAVOR?

I DO NOT UNDERSTAND. ALL THESE THINGS ARE HARD AND COLD...NOT GOOD TO EAT. BUT I WOULD TAKE THIS WITH ME THAT I MAY SEE IT SHINE IN THE SUN. WILL YOU GIVE IT TO ME? I WILL BRING YOU FROGS TO EAT IN EXCHANGE.

MANLING LOOK AT YOUR FEET!

THEY CAME TO TAKE THE TREASURE AWAY. I SPOKE TO THEM AND THEY LAY STILL! NO MAN TAKES ANYTHING FROM THIS VAULT!

BUT I HAVE NO QUARREL WITH YOU... AND I WAS TAUGHT THE MASTER WORD OF YOUR TRIBE.

IF YOU BUT MOVE FROM THIS PLACE WITH THE POINTED THING...YOU DIE!

AFTER THEY HAD LEFT THE COLD LAIRS, KAA WENT OFF TO HUNT AND MOWGLI WENT TO FIND BAGHEERA. TO TELL HIM THE STORY AND ASK HIM ABOUT THE WARNING WORDS OF THE COBRA...

AH, BAGHEERA, I HAVE A TALE TO TELL YOU.

AND MOWGLI TOLD THE WHOLE STORY. WHEN HE CAME TO THE END...

AND THE WHITE HOOD SAID "IT IS DEATH! IT IS DEATH!" HOW CAN THIS THING KILL BAGHEERA?

I HAVE LIVED AMONG MEN AND I TELL YOU, MOWGLI, THE WHITE HOOD SPOKE THE TRUTH. MEN WOULD KILL THRICE IN A NIGHT FOR THE BIG RED STONE ALONE!

BUT THE RED STONE IS NOT GOOD TO EAT! WHY SHOULD THEY KILL? IF THIS THING DRAWS BLOOD, I WANT NONE OF IT.

SEE! NOW MY HANDS ARE CLEAN OF DEATH! BUT THE WHITE HOOD SAID DEATH WOULD FOLLOW! HE IS OLD AND MAD!

THE NEXT MORNING, MOWGLI WENT TO TAKE A LAST LOOK AT THE POINTED THING...

WHERE IS THE THORN-POINTED THING?

A MAN HAS TAKEN IT. HERE IS HIS TRAIL.

NOW WE SHALL SEE WHETHER FATHER COBRA SPOKE THE TRUTH. IF THE POINTED THING IS DEATH, THAT MAN WILL DIE. WILL IT TURN IN THE MAN'S HANDS AND KILL HIM?

WE SHALL SEE. MAN USES SUCH THINGS TO THRUST INTO THE HEADS OF THE SONS OF HATHI, THE ELEPHANT...BUT NEVER AGAINST HIMSELF!

THIS TRAIL IS AS PLAIN AS SUMMER LIGHTNING.

WHY DOES HE TURN A-SIDE HERE?

WAIT! I SHALL SEE IF I CAN FIND THE ANSWER!

WHEN A TRAIL CEASES TO EXPLAIN ITSELF, THE FIRST THING THE JUNGLE FOLK DO IS TO CAST THEMSELVES FORWARD AS FAR AS THEY CAN...TO SEE IF THERE IS SOMETHING HIDDEN FROM THEM, AND TO KEEP FROM CONFUSING THE TRAIL WITH THEIR OWN FOOTPRINTS.

HERE COMES ANOTHER MAN TO MEET HIM! IT IS A SMALLER FOOT. A LITTLE HUNTER. HE DRAGS A BOW AND ARROW.

HEAR HIM! WE MUST LEAVE OUR HUNTING GROUNDS...OUR HOMES...OUR RIVER TO THE DHOLE...AND WHEN IT SO PLEASES THEM, AFTER THEY HAVE RUINED OUR LAND, THEN WE CAN SNEAK HOME! I SAY...NO! *WE MUST FIGHT!*

TO THE DEATH!

TO THE DEATH!

I GO TO COUNT THE DHOLE.

*S*UDDENLY HE STUMBLED...

WHAT SORT OF STAMP-ING AND UNMANNERLY TRAMPING IS THIS, LITTLE BROTHER?

KAA!

"THE BUCK LIVED!"

MM...SO THE BUCK LIVED!

YES, LITTLE BROTHER. HE LIVED BECAUSE HE CAME FIRST, AND LEAPED BEFORE THE LITTLE PEOPLE WERE AWARE. WHEN THE PACK CAME, THE BEES WERE ALREADY GATHERED FOR THE KILL... NOW, WHAT IS YOUR PLAN?

IT IS TO PULL THE VERY WHISKERS OF DEATH, O KAA! TELL THE PACK I BRING THE DHOLE DOWNSTREAM AFTER ME...THEN YOU COME BACK AND WAIT FOR ME!

KAA FLASHED DOWNSTREAM TO DELIVER MOWGLI'S MESSAGE...

HUSH, DOGS! THE DHOLE WILL COME DOWN-STREAM. IF YOU BE NOT AFRAID, YOU CAN KILL THEM IN THE SHALLOWS.

WHERE IS MY MAN-CUB?

WHEN WILL THEY COME?

THEY COME WHEN THEY COME! WAIT FOR THEM! AS FOR YOUR MAN-CUB, HE IS SAFE WITH ME! WAIT HERE FOR THE DHOLE AND BE THANKFUL WE ARE ON YOUR SIDE!

...AND THROUGH THE JUNGLE, MOWGLI SPED, LOOKING FOR THE DHOLE...

SUDDENLY, HE STOOPED...

THE OUTLIER'S TRAIL! THE DHOLE WILL BE FOLLOWING IT... THIS WILL LEAD ME TO THEM!

FOR TWO MILES, MOWGLI FOLLOWED THE OUTLIER'S TRAIL, UNTIL...

THIS TREE SUITS ME.

HAH! GARLIC! THIS MAY BE OF HELP LATER!

THEN HE CLIMBED INTO THE TREE AND WAITED...

SOON, HE HEARD THE PATTER OF MANY FEET...

...AND AROUND A BEND IN THE TRAIL CAME THE DHOLE LEADER...

GOOD HUNTING!

SUDDENLY, THE LEADER, FURIOUS, SHOT UP CLOSE TO MOWGLI AND...

MOWGLI CUT THE DHOLE LEADER'S TAIL CLEAR THROUGH, LEAVING THE VICIOUS ANIMAL WITH MERELY A STUB. MOWGLI THEN LET THE "RED DOG" DROP BACK TO THE GROUND AND PROCEEDED TO TAUNT THE PACK BY WAVING THE LEADER'S TAIL OVER THEIR HEADS.

THIS, OF COURSE, ENRAGED THE PACK MORE THAN EVER...

WE'LL NOT MOVE FROM HERE UNTIL YOU DIE!

...AT LAST HE CAME TO THE EDGE OF THE FOREST. HE THEN RUBBED HIMSELF CAREFULLY WITH GARLIC.

APE WITH THE WOLF'S TONGUE! DO YOU THINK TO COVER YOUR SCENT? WE FOLLOW YOU TO THE DEATH!

TAKE YOUR TAIL...

...AND FOLLOW NOW TO THE DEATH!

SOON MOWGLI WAS AT THE EDGE OF THE CLIFF.

...AND MOWGLI LEAPED INTO THE RIVER...

REPELLED BY THE GARLIC SMELL, THE AWAKENED BEES FLEW AWAY FROM MOWGLI TOWARD THE DOGS.

THIS IS NO PLACE FOR US! THE LITTLE PEOPLE ARE ANGRY INDEED! COME!

DIVING TO KEEP AWAY FROM THE BEES, MOWGLI SWAM...KNIFE IN HAND READY FOR THE FIGHT...

THE BEES FOLLOWED DOWN-STREAM...

HEAR THEM HOWL!

WHERE IS THE TREE APE?

LET ME GET MY TEETH INTO HIM!

THE JUNGLE BOOK
RUDYARD KIPLING

Rudyard Kipling (1865-1936) is one of the most popular story-tellers in the English language. His novels, short stories, poems, and children's books have entertained readers for more than a hundred years, and although his reputation as a writer of serious literature has fluctuated greatly, he has always retained an audience of devoted readers, many of whom discovered him as a child and continued to read him throughout life. Although in his lifetime Kipling was famous in the literary world for his short stories, and became a best-selling writer of poetry, he found his greatest audience in his children's stories. Today, he's remembered for his many dozens of excellent short stories as well as for a handful of famous poems—the best-known is probably "Gunga Din"—but his most enduring work seems to be his books for children, including *Kim*, *Just So Stories*, *Captains Courageous*, and, above all, *The Jungle Books*.

The Author

Rudyard Kipling was born in Bombay, India, on December 30th, 1865, the son of middle-class English parents who were involved in the fine arts. John Kipling was a designer and aspiring painter, and two of his wife's sisters married famous painters; although the family was not

wealthy or prominent, it was well connected with the art world, which was considered very respectable in Victorian England. A few years before Rudyard's birth, John Kipling took a job at an art school in Bombay, and later became curator of a Lahore museum. Although it wasn't an especially prestigious or well-paying position by British standards, in colonial India an Englishman with a middle-class job could live very well, and Rudyard and his younger sister grew up surrounded by servants. The children learned to speak the native dialect better than they spoke English, and spent their first years happily immersed in the temples, market-places, and hills of India.

At this time India was part of the British Empire (one of Queen Victoria's many titles was "Empress of India"); countries all over the world, including Canada, Australia, Singapore, and Hong Kong, were either protectorates or colonies of Great Britain. India, an empire that had been overrun by invaders in the eighteenth century and had fragmented into squabbling kingdoms, was a land wracked with disease, periodic famine, and great social injustice. England, which had been engaged in active trade with India since the 1600s, decided by the end of the eighteenth century that the threat to trade created by political instability could only be solved if India was brought under British control. By 1818 India was united as a single political entity within the British Empire.

Unfortunately for Kipling, the Indian climate was considered unhealthy for English children; when Rudyard was six he and his younger sister Trix were taken back to England to live. This was common practice for Anglo-Indian families; such children were usually sent to live with aunts and uncles or grand-parents. But Rudyard and Trix were sent to live in the house of strangers who had advertised their willingness to care for others' children. The two siblings spent six miserable years there, unloved and ill-treated, especially Rudyard, who was bullied and beaten by the severely religious woman who ran the household. He developed eye problems which went untreated, and nearly lost his sight. By the time his mother returned on a visit and discovered how the children were being treated, he had suffered a kind of nervous breakdown, and was emotionally scarred by the experience for the rest of his life.

At twelve, Kipling went to boarding school, an inexpensive insti-tution for the sons of officers, who were expected to go on to military academies rather than to Oxford or Cambridge. Kipling, who loved liter-ature and had no intention of entering the army or navy, was rather a misfit at this school, but after initially suf-fering more bullying at the hands of his classmates (a fictionalized account of his school years can be found in his novel *Stalky & Co.*) he found his place there, as a bookish,

decidedly *un*athletic boy in an athlet-ic, *un*bookish school.

Despite this, Kipling received a good education, although his parents couldn't afford to send him to col-lege. At the age of seventeen he returned to India, where he took a job as a reporter at a newspaper in Lahore, the capital of the district of Punjab.

It was as a journalist in Lahore that Kipling developed his skills as a writer and a careful observer, and began writing his first stories. His earliest work comprised very short stories about contemporary life among the English colonists, which filled up leftover space in the news-paper. But Kipling kept his eyes and ears open, and saw a great deal of the world of colonial India—not just the privileged world of the English busi-nessmen and administrators, but also the world of the common English sol-diers, and that of the Indians them-selves. He published *Departmental Ditties*, a book of light verse, when he was twenty. In 1888, when Kipling was twenty-two, he published a short collection of stories, *Plain Tales from the Hills*. The book was a success, and Kipling published sever-al more collections that year. When he arrived in London the following year, word had preceded him that a remarkable young Anglo-Indian writer had appeared on the literary scene; and with the republication of his stories in England, Kipling became famous.

Over the next two years Kipling travelled widely, married, and settled down with his American-born wife in Vermont. It is here that he began to write stories for children, which gained

The British in India

The thousands of Englishmen who lived in India during the years of Kipling's youth were there for many reasons. Most were involved in some way with the immense trade that went on between the two countries—India was a market for British textiles and other exports, and a profitable source of silk, spices, and minerals—but many were missionaries, intent on educating the Indians and introducing them to Christianity, or teachers, or doctors; and thousands of others were engineers, assigned to build railroads, bridges, dams, and other projects on the vast undeveloped sub-continent.

Although many of the Englishman in India were motivated purely by profit, and most were convinced of the racial superiority of the European over the Indian, a great number of these people felt the impulse to try to help the Indian people, who were the product of an old and highly developed civilization but who lived, for the most part, in disease and material want. The British outlawed such venerable Indian practices as *suttee* (the burning of widows on their husbands'

funeral pyres) and sought—largely without success—to abolish its caste system and its religious strife. Although Kipling had little interest in missionary work, he felt a great sympathy for the Englishmen who attempted—often at the risk of great personal hardship and danger—to help build India's roads and bridges and to bring the Victorian values of hard work, respect for authority, and self-improvement to the native cultures in India and elsewhere. Kipling placed a great value on technical skills, and his stories lauded the men who had mastered their crafts—ship's captains, mining engineers, artillerymen—and worked hard at them.

him a second audience, even greater than those who had read his tales of life in Imperial India, and he became rich. In rapid succession Kipling wrote *The Jungle Book*, *The Second Jungle Book,* an early draft of *Kim* (his only novel set in India), and *Captains Courageous*. After four years Kipling returned to England, where (although he continued to travel) he lived for the rest of his long life.

In the first years of the new century, Kipling published *Kim* and the *Just So Stories*, his only books for children that can rival the *The Jungle Book* in enduring popularity. In 1907 he won the Nobel Prize for Literature, the youngest writer ever to do so. His poetry, which was collected in *Barrack-Room Ballads* and other volumes, was extremely popular.

But this wasn't a happy period for him personally: his eldest daughter died, and Kipling quarrelled with his American in-laws, making it impossible to live any longer in America. He became a friend of Cecil Rhodes and other British imperialists in South Africa, and spoke out unwisely in support of imperialism, often in ways that made him sound bigoted and jingoistic. Kipling's most famous poem, "The White Man's Burden," which champions the European's mission to civilize the populations of what is today called the Third World (populations whom Kipling referred to as "Your new-caught, sullen peoples, Half devil and half child"), offered a sentiment that had been popular during the Victorian era, but which, in the years leading up to World War I, seemed irrelevant to the new century, and offensive to many. Kipling's son was killed in World War I, and the remaining years of his life were largely unhappy.

Yet they were creative years. Kipling published only a few novels in his lifetime, and none after *Kim* in 1901. For the rest of his career he concentrated primarily on short stories, the form he had mastered as a young man. Although he lost a good deal of the critical acclaim he had enjoyed in his early years—his politics put him increasingly out of step with the times—many critics now believe that the stories he published during his last twenty years are among his finest. Kipling's love of technology and expertise, and his concern for the future, led him to write a number of science fiction stories, as well as the ghost stories, fantasies, and stories of contemporary life that he had always written.

Kipling died in January, 1936, shortly after his seventieth birthday. He was buried in Westminster Cathedral, an honor reserved for England's greatest writers.

The Original "Jungle Book"
Kipling published *The Jungle Book* in 1894, after first publishing several of the stories in magazines. Three of the stories—"Mowgli's Brothers," "The King's Ankus," and "Tiger-Tiger!"—dealt with Mowgli the Frog, while the others were animal stories, told from the point of view of the animal. The best-known of these, "Rikki-Tikki-Tavi," is also set in colonial India, and tells the story of Rikki-Tikki-Tavi, a young mongoose who is adopted as a pet by a British boy and ends up saving the boy's family from the attacks of two

deadly cobras. In addition, Kipling included a poem after each story, usually a "song" that one of the story's characters might have made up. This unusual practice became a trademark for Kipling, and he continued it in most of his short story collections. (See "Hunting-Song of the Seeonee Pack" below.)

The Jungle Book was so successful that Kipling published *The Second Jungle Book* a year later. Five of the eight tales in this volume also feature Mowgli, whose story is brought to a conclusion in them. After "Red Dog," the most action-filled of the series, the last story is "Spring Running," in which Mowgli, now nearly seventeen, faces up to the fact that he will have to return to the village and live with humankind. It is a melancholy conclusion, but one which was foreshadowed from the very first story. At the end of it, Kipling wrote: "And this is the last of the Mowgli stories."

Although only half the stories in the two *The Jungle Books* (the two volumes are usually published together in modern editions) deal with Mowgli, his story dominates both volumes. There have been at least four films called "The Jungle Book" (a 1942 British version, the famous animated feature made by Walt Disney in 1967, and two live-action versions released in the Nineties), and all of them star Mowgli. If you ask most adult readers what they remember about *The Jungle Book*, they're likely to reply, "It's the story of Mowgli, the boy who was raised by wolves."

In 1897 Kipling published a uniform edition of his work, and in it he assembled all the Mowgli stories together and called that volume *The Jungle Book*. He added a final story,

THE CUB MUST BE SHOWN TO THE PACK. WILL YOU KEEP HIM?

ASSUREDLY! MOWGLI, THE FROG, WILL I CALL YOU! YES, ONE DAY YOU SHALL HUNT SHERE KAHN AS HE HAS HUNTED YOU!

"In the Rukh," which shows Mowgli as a grown man, now living in the *rukh* (the jungle) and bemusing the Englishman who works as the park ranger. Interestingly, this story was written in 1893, *before* Kipling began work on *The Jungle Book*. He already knew Mowgli as an adult (although not one who actually spoke with animals) before he decided to make him a child raised in the jungle by animals.

Readers who look up the Mowgli stories may also wish to look at *The Jungle Book* as Kipling first published it, with three Mowgli stories—not the first three in terms of the story's chronology, nor the three included in this Classics Illustrated edition—included with other stories. But the story of *The Jungle Book*, despite these other stories, is essentially the story of Mowgli the feral child.

TABLE OF CONTENTS OF *THE JUNGLE BOOK*

THREE STORIES FROM *THE JUNGLE BOOK*
"Mowgli's Brothers"

"Mowgli's Brothers" tells the story of Mowgli's appearance as an infant wandering in the jungles of the Seeonee Hills in central India, and how Mother Wolf decides to keep him when he fearlessly pushes his way among her cubs to nurse from her. Kipling quickly introduces his cast—in addition to Mother Wolf, Father Wolf, and their cubs, there is Shere Khan, the tiger who claims Mowgli as his prey; Akela, the leader of the wolves; Baloo, the bear who teaches young wolves the Law of the Jungle; and Bagheera, the panther who buys Mowgli with the price of a fresh-killed bull.

In the space of ten pages (five in the Classics Illustrated adaptation), Kipling introduces virtually all his major characters; only one, Kaa the python, is not brought swiftly on stage.

The "Law of the Jungle"—otherwise referred to simply as "the Law"—lies at the center of the story. At first glance, it may seem that the Law is simply a plot device—a pretext that gives the wolves and Shere Khan something to argue over—but in fact the Law is central to all of the Mowgli stories: indeed, it is central to all of Kipling's work.

"To kill a naked cub is shame,"

says Bagheera, expressing a sentiment that, if it is not actually part of the Law, seems to carry great moral force. Another rule is the injunction against killing cattle, which turns out to be bad when Shere Khan does it, but all right when Bagheera does it. In "Kaa's Hunting" (not included here), we learn that the monkeys live "outside the Law," and are regarded with disdain and moral distaste by every other Jungle creature. These attitudes seem peculiar to today's readers, whose ideas of life in the animal kingdom are likely to be influenced by their appreciation of ecological balance, in which every creature plays a role in the complex web of a region's ecology, with none of the roles being "shameful" or "ignoble." The "Circle of Life" (as it's called in the Disney movie *The Lion King*) is not the concept that underlies Kipling's view of nature.

But Kipling's view of nature in *The Jungle Book* is a vision of the jungle as a replica of human society—with its natural leaders, its riff-raff, and its dishonorable elements, which are always threatening to sully the rest. In Kipling's jungle, every creature does not have an ecological niche that fills an important purpose: some niches are simply detestable. Thus Tabaqui the jackal, who eats the leftover kills of tigers and wolves, is a "miserable" creature and a "dish-licker," regarded as a flunkey and treated with disdain by both the Free People

and Kipling himself. (In fairness, the hyenas in *The Lion King* are presented as odious as well. Carrion-eaters are sufficiently unappealing to human sensibilities that even a movie which embraces "the circle of life" can't help but present them as loathesome.)

More interesting is the portrayal of Shere Khan, the tiger who was hunting Mowgli when he found shelter with the wolves and who continues to claim him as his prey. In the Disney version of *The Jungle Book*, Shere Khan is presented as frightening but regal; his powerful bearing and upper-class British accent show that while he's an enemy he is not a villain. Kipling, however, does not acknowledge the concept of an "honorable enemy;" since the Jungle is an integrated society, any enemy within it must be a treacherous one. Thus Shere Khan is portrayed in relentlessly negative terms—not simply a predator who is making it his business to hunt prey, but a disruptive and hateful figure.

It is particularly interesting to note that Shere Khan is lame, and the fact that he has been lame from birth is used to explain why he sometimes hunts cattle, and even—as Mother Wolf at one point disdainfully notes—frogs and fish. (See image on next page). (Kipling makes it clear that a hunter who eats such fare is low indeed). A modern reader tends to feel more sympathy for a creature that is forced by circumstances to

engage in behavior that would otherwise be beneath his dignity. For Kipling, Shere Khan's lameness is another sign of his unworthiness; at times Kipling seems to show a marked antipathy for weakness and those who are weak.

Given that Shere Khan the Tiger and Tabaqui that Jackal seem to have no place in the Jungle even when they obey the rule of "the Law," it is not surprising that they serve in the story

stances, the only dramatic possibilities open to the author are either a story about the Law being upheld or a story of the Law being dishonored, and there is no question which alternative makes for a more interesting story.

"Mowgli's Brothers" is a very bitter tale, an account of how the young wolves of the Free People fail to follow the ways of their elder leader Akela, listening instead to Shere Khan. The tiger seduces and corrupts them, allowing them to eat his scraps, then persuades them to contrive Akela's overthrow. (This last detail is not included in the Classics Illustrated adaptation.) When the young wolves gain control of the pack, they repudiate Mowgli's membership among the Free People, a disgraceful act.

essentially as betrayers of that Law. For Kipling, adherence to "the Law" is an absolute requirement; and the Law is neither to be questioned or changed. Under such circum-

Mowgli's denunciation of them—a magnificent tirade in which he calls them "dogs" rather than "brothers"—passes unforgiving judgment on a people who have fallen from the Law. "I see that ye are dogs," he comments after frightening them with the fire:

"I go from you to my own people—if they be my own people. The Jungle is shut to me, and I must forget your talk and your companionship; but I will be more merciful than ye are. Because I was all but brother in blood, I promise that when I am a man

among men I will not betray ye to men as ye have betrayed me."

Mowgli beats Shere Khan and drives him away, then concludes by telling the terrified wolves that they won't kill Akela, "because that is not my will. Nor do I think that ye will sit here any longer, lolling out your tongues as though ye were somebodies, instead of dogs whom I drive out—thus! Go!"

To lapse from observance of the Law thus causes one to forfeit forever all honor and respect. Mowgli makes clear that in turning on him, the pack has made itself unworthy of his company. The only alternative to the Law is treachery and degradation; and Mowgli turns toward the world of men because the Free People are now beneath him.

Such an unyielding, unforgiving view of "animal" behavior (Kipling is of course talking about human behavior) is almost guaranteed to bring disappointment: although Kipling was a young and extremely successful man when he wrote *The Jungle Book*, one could almost predict that he would in time turn into the angry political reactionary he indeed became.

"Mowgli's Brothers" also tells another story: the story of childhood's end, how one must turn painfully away from the enclosed and nurturing world of one's early happiness—what the British poet A.E. Housman called "the land of lost content"—in order to enter adulthood. The emotion that suddenly sweeps over Mowgli immediately after he drives away the young wolves in the pack is unexpected and, given the spirit of revenge that has prevailed up till now, surprisingly affecting:

Mowgli struck right and left round the circle, and the wolves ran howling with the sparks burning their fur. At last there were only Akela, Bagheera, and perhaps ten wolves that had taken Mowgli's part. Then something began to hurt Mowgli inside him, as he had never been hurt in his life before, and he caught his breath and sobbed, and the tears ran down his face. "What is it? What is it?" he said. "I do not wish to leave the Jungle, and I do not know what this is. Am I dying, Bagheera?"

"No, Little Brother. Those are only tears such as men use," said Bagheera. "Now I know thou art a man, and a man's cub no longer. The Jungle is shut indeed to thee thenceforward. Let them fall, Mowgli. They are only tears." So Mowgli sat and cried as though his heart would burst; and he had never cried in all his life before.

The story of a society that fails to adhere rigidly to a codified set of laws and consequently falls into barbarism is usually an old man's tale, while the story of youth's painful initiation into adulthood is certainly a young man's tale. For Kipling to succeed in telling both stories at once is one of the peculiar triumphs of "Mowgli's Brothers." Mowgli is not only adult and child at once; he also prefigures the old man that Kipling would in time become, just as the story of what happens to the Free People when they stray from the Law of the Jungle can be read as a prophetic warning (from the imperialist's point of view) of what might befall India if it frees itself from England's stern yet benevolent rule.

"The King's Ankus"

"The King's Ankus" (the fifth of the Mowgli stories, although the second one in the Classics Illustrated adaptation) is a very different story from "Mowgli's Brothers." While the earlier story combined fantasy with elements of fable, "The King's Ankus" is more like a science fiction story.

The tale of a long-vanished civilization, a guardian that has lost track of the passage of time, and a cultural

artifact that is incomprehensible to its finder, "The King's Ankus" could be

transferred, element by element, into a story set in the far future, where lost technologies and immortal watchkeepers who have long outlived their era lie beneath the site of an extinct alien civilization. The wonder that Mowgli feels when he realizes that the ancient cobra does not know that the city above him has fallen into ruin is a sentiment that can only be felt by a modern sensibility. "Mowgli's Brothers" is a story that

can take place in any era—its setting is an Eden before the Fall, and its events could as easily have happened in the days of the Roman gods as in the nineteenth century—while "The King's Ankus" stands late in the long perspective of history.

The story falls into two halves, the first set in the vault beneath the lost city, and the second dealing with the ankus (an ankus is an elephant goad, used to jab a tame elephant into action) after Mowgli takes it back to the Jungle. Although the first part feels modern, the second part is very old: the tale of the thieves who murder one another (with the last ones eating a poisoned meal that the thief they had earlier murdered had prepared for them) is taken from Geoffrey Chaucer's "The Pardoner's Tale," one of the *Canterbury Tales*, written in the 1390s.

There are other echoes of medieval English literature in *The Jungle Book*; "Rikki-Tikki-Tavi," the tale of a brave mongoose that saves the family who takes it in, is in many respects a retelling of "Beowulf," a ninth century Old English epic of a warrior who slays the monster Grendel and then descends underground to battle his deadly mother. Kipling had a great reverence for English literature, especially anything from Shakespeare's day or earlier, and probably created these parallels as a conscious *homage*, knowing that his readers would encounter the originals when they were a few years older and recognize what he had done.

Critic Angus Wilson believed that "The crown of the two books is 'The King's Ankus,' Kipling's best use of myth in all his work." He notes that the story begins with Edenic happiness, as Mowgli and Kaa rest pleasantly by a jungle pool.

When the contented boy muses, "What more can I wish? I have the Jungle and the favor of the Jungle. Is there anything more between sunrise and sunset?" Kaa—who is after all a serpent—whispers into Mowgli's ear the knowledge of something new. The knowledge of greed and what men will do for wealth comes as the Apple of Knowledge that signals Mowgli's expulsion from Eden: even though he returns the ankus to the vault and the impotent cobra (also a serpent), he retains the knowledge of what Man is capable of.

This does not, at the moment, matter to Mowgli: he does not consider himself a man. The reader knows, however, that he will someday learn better.

"Red Dog"

"Red Dog" is the seventh Mowgli story, and with the death of the aged Akela at its conclusion, it signals that the end of the series is near. In "The Spring Running," the last tale, Mowgli must face up to his return to the world of human beings at last.

Thus, "Red Dog" is kind of a

last hurrah for Mowgli. Most of his stories have been adventures, with Mowgli being captured by monkeys, having a final encounter with Shere Khan, and making an early, unhappy attempt to live among humans. "The Spring Running" has almost no action in it; its tone is mournful and bittersweet. The adventure Mowgli undertakes in "Red Dog" is his last and greatest exploit.

Like many of the Mowgli stories, "Red Dog" is a tale of successful revenge. Kipling's early books are often stories about protagonists avenging themselves, and are fre-

THE DHOLE'...RED DOG, THE KILLER! THEY CAME WHEN THE MOON WAS NEW...KILLED MY MATE AND THREE CUBS...THEN I TRAILED THEM...

'A WILD DOG'

quently told with a kind of glee that make modern readers feel a bit uneasy. (When Mowgli hears that Shere Khan is conspiring with the young wolves against him, he declares, "I will pay Shere Khan full tale for this, and it may be a little over." He does, too.) We have already mentioned Kipling's tendency to insist that the natural doings of one or another type of animal are dishonorable or evil, and the relish with which he describes their eventual comeuppance. The tale of the Jungle's invasion by the dhole or "red dog" (Kipling once more presents the dog

Hunting—The Song of the Seeonee Pack
(From The Jungle Book)

As the dawn was breaking the Sambhur belled —
> Once, twice and again!
And a doe leaped up and a doe leaped up
From the pond in the wood where the wild deer sup.
This I, scouting alone, beheld,
> Once, twice and again!

As the dawn was breaking the Sambhur belled —
> Once, twice and again!
And a wolf stole back, and a wolf stole back
To carry the word to the waiting pack,
And we sought and we found and we bayed on his track
> Once, twice and again!

As the dawn was breaking the Sambhur belled —
> Once, twice and again!
Feet in the jungle that leave no mark!
Eyes that can see in the dark—the dark!
Tongue—give tongue to it! Hark! O hark!
> Once, twice and again!

Books by Rudyard Kipling

The Jungle Book, 1894. Seven stories, only three of which deal with Mowgli. The others include "Rikki-Tikki-Tavi," perhaps Kipling's greatest story for young readers.

The Second Jungle Book, 1895. The rest of the Mowgli stories, plus several others. (Some editions of the *The Jungle Book* gather the Mowgli stories into one volume.)

Kim, 1902. Kipling's finest novel, and one of the best novels for young readers in English. Its portrayal of life in colonial India is unsurpassed.

Just So Stories, 1903. Stories—such as "How the Leopard Got His Spots" and "The Elephant Child"—for younger children. Their charm and myth-like simplicity have made this book a classic.

Kipling's Science Fiction, 1992. New York: Tor Books. Introduction by John Brunner. A good collection of Kipling's science fiction stories.

Kipling's Fantasy Stories, 1992. New York: Tor Books. Introduction by John Brunner. A collection of Kipling's fantasies for adults, including some of his best work.

Collected Stories, 1994. New York: Modern Library. Selected and edited by Robert Gottleib.

Despite its title, this does not contain all of Kipling's short stories, but at more than 800 pages, it is the largest selection available in one volume.

Books about Rudyard Kipling

Harrison, James. *Rudyard Kipling*. Boston: Twayne Publishers, 1982. A short and very good introduction to Kipling's life and works.

Orwell, George. *Dickens, Dali & Others*. New York: Harcourt Brace, 1946. (Available as a Harvest paperback.) Contains his famous essay, "Rudyard Kipling."

Wilson, Angus. *The Strange Ride of Rudyard Kipling*. New York: Viking, 1977. A good critical biography of Kipling.

---

as an ignoble inferior of the wolf) is his most spectacular story of destruction visited on those outside "the Law."

As an exciting tale, "Red Dog" can hardly be bettered. The dhole pack is portrayed as a plague, a locust-like invasion that can't be halted or turned aside. In order to execute his plan, Mowgli must put himself directly in the path of the pack, then goad it into a fury against him, so that it will pursue him in the direction he wants. This scene, with

Mowgli dangling from a tree as he taunts the dogs into a murderous frenzy, is great drama; but Kipling is able to achieve an even greater dramatic effect from a scene that contains no action whatsoever, when he describes the "Place of Death" where the "Little People"—the wild bees—live:

The length of the gorge on both sides was hung as it were with black shimmery velvet curtains, and Mowgli sank as he looked, for those were the clot-

ted millions of the sleeping bees. There were other lumps and festoons and things like decayed tree-trunks studded on the face of the rock, the old combs of past years, or new cities built in the shadow of the windless gorge, and huge masses of spongy, rotten trash had rolled down and stuck among the trees and creepers that clung to the rock-face. As he listened he heard more than once the rustle and slide of a honey-loaded comb turning over and falling away somewhere in the dark galleries; then a booming of angry wings, and the sullen drip, drip, drip, of the wasted honey, guttering along till it lipped over some ledge in the open air and sluggishly trickled down on the twigs.

If "The King's Ankus" was similar in many respects to science fiction, "Red Dog" is—in this scene, anyway—something of a horror story. The gorge where the Little People live is described as though it were a living organism, with oozing bodily fluids, mysterious sounds emerging from cavities within, and its wastes lying scattered around it.

The preoccupation Kipling has shown throughout *The Jungle Book* as to "Who is Master of the Jungle?"—is it Kaa, or Hathi the Elephant, or Mowgli himself, or the fearsome dhole?—is finally answered: the true Master of the Jungle is the terrifying creature that is the Little People.

These two scenes, then, portray respectively a hateful menace and a deadly, invincible sleeping monster: Kipling then does the natural thing, and has Mowgli throw one up against the other. The scene in which Mogli runs into the gorge of the Little People, with two hundred dhole baying behind him, and dives into the river just as the bees awake in their angry millions is perhaps the most exciting of the series. In some ways it's almost *too* exciting: in the first part of his climax, in which the dhole are attacked by the bees, Kipling shifts into a heightened, almost hallucinogenic prose:

...AND MOWGLI LEAPED INTO THE RIVER.

Some of the dholes, too, had fallen into the gullies that communicated with the underground caves, and there choked and fought and snapped among the tumbled honeycombs, and at last, borne up, even when they were dead, on the heaving waves of bees beneath them, shot out of some hole in the river-face, to roll over on the black rubbish-heaps.

The image of the dogs' bodies bobbing along on a surf of swarming bees is so utterly over the top that the reader is astonished. This surreal tone continues in the scene's second half, as the surviving dholes are swept downstream to crawl ashore, soaked and exhausted, to be slaughtered by the Free People. Kipling's uncharacteristic use of heightened imagery continues: Won-Tolla, the wolf whose family has been killed by the dhole, is seen capering with joy at the sight of the dholes' plight—"as though he were playing with his cubs," Kipling notes with mordant irony—and in a page-and-a half-long paragraph, the pitch of his prose rises to the breaking point:

SUDDENLY MOWGLI HEARD THE OUTLIER SNARL IN TRIUMPH...

BY THE GREAT GULL THAT BOUGHT ME, THE OUTLIER HAS THE TAILLESS ONE!

> *Here would be a heaving mound, like a water-blister in a whirlpool, which would break like a water-blister, and throw up four or five mangled dogs, each striving to get back to the centre; here would be a single wolf borne down by two or three dholes, laboriously dragging them forward, and sinking the while; here a yearling cub would be held up by the pressure round him, though he had been killed early, while his mother, crazed with dumb rage, rolled over and over, snapping, and passing on and in the middle of the thickest press, perhaps, one wolf and one dhole, forgetting everything else, would be manoeuvring for first hold till they were whirled away by a rush of furious fighters.*

In the end, Mowgli and Won-Tolla together find themselves fighting the leader of the dholes, whose tail Mowgli had earlier cut off; and Mowgli gets another chance to mock the badly injured dhole before it dies.

It's impossible to overlook the sadistic pleasure that Kipling is taking in these scenes. Mowgli generally exults when he revenges himself on someone who has broken the Law or lives outside it, and the reader is invited to share his triumph. The dhole are plainly hated because they're outsiders: "He despised and hated them because because they did not smell like the Free People, because they did not live in caves, and above all, because they had hair between their toes while he and his friends were clean-footed." This sounds like a straightforward description of Mowgli's aversion to unfamiliar creatures (a normal characteristic in one who lives in a pack), but when he taunts the dhole by wiggling his toes at them, Kipling explains that "Those who have hair between their toes do not care to be reminded of it." It is a feature of Kipling's Jungle that the prejudices Mowgli and his friends have against certain creatures are shared by the creatures themselves: the monkeys crave the good opinion that the Jungle's hunters deny them, and the dhole recognize their hairy toes as a sign of racial inferiority. The triumph Mowgli feels in seeing the dholes (or Shere Khan, or the monkeys who kidnap him in "Kaa's Hunting") destroyed is one Kipling thinks the reader should sympathize with.

The destruction of the dhole, in fact, is total: when Mowgli sees that Won-Tolla has died of his wounds, he calls for the dhole's utter destruction: "Pay the debt! They have slain the Lone Wolf! Let not a dog go!" And as Kipling grandly relates in the story's last sentence, the Free People succeed in killing every single dhole. It is, in short, a massacre, and modern readers shouldn't feel uneasy at finding themselves unable to respond to the annihilation of one population by another in the way that Kipling means them to.

BAGHEERA TAUGHT HIM TO CLIMB...

feral children has had an unending fascination for readers, whether they are themselves children or adults. Edgar Rice Burrough's Tarzan, possibly the most famous literary character of the twentieth century, was a feral child—and probably owes something in his inspiration to Mowgli.

Surprisingly, such stories seem to have some basis in fact: although a child abandoned in the wilderness seems almost certain to perish of exposure or be eaten, evidence from around the world suggests that, on rare occasions, such castaways have indeed been nurtured by animals. The case of "Peter the Wild Boy," a child discovered in the forests of Hanover, Germany, in 1825, was famous throughout Europe; and the case of "Victor," discovered in a French forest, was studied scientifically in 1798 (the story became the basis of François Truffaut's 1970 film "The Wild Child").

The Allure of the Wild Child

The child who has been raised by animals—otherwise called a "feral child" or "wild child"—has been a recurrent figure in folklore for thousands of years. Ancient Romans used to claim that their city was founded by Romulus and Remus, two infants who were raised by a she-wolf, and tales of young children lost in the wilderness and raised by animals (usually wolves) appear in the stories of European, Asian, and Native American cultures. In modern times the idea of

Documented cases in which a lost child was actually succored by animals are much rarer. In the eighteenth century a "wild boy" was discovered living with bears in a forest of Lithuania; and in a well-known case, a six-year-old boy living on the Canadian prairie wandered away from his family in 1870 and was adopted for several months by a badger that had evidently lost its young.

The best-known case, however, took place in India in 1920. A hunting expedition discovered two young girls living in a wolf's den with a mother wolf and her cubs. Nobody could determine the age of the girls, who could not talk or walk upright, or discover how long they had lived there. The girls were taken to an orphanage, where they behaved in the manner of wolves: running on all fours, eating raw meat, gnawing bones, and refusing to wear clothing. One of the girls died within the year, but the other one, named Kamala, lived for nine years at the orphanage, where teachers struggled to assimilate her into human society. It was three years before Kamala learned to walk or began to speak, and she never became fluent with speech. She died in 1929, without ever having learned to speak well enough to tell how she came to be living among wolves.

The feral child is a figure that, paradoxically, combines both freedom and obligation: He (it is almost always a "he" in fiction) is free of the bonds of human society, but constrained by the bonds of another society— that of the animals who raised him: a society to which he can't truly belong. The figure of Mowgli, living naked and wild in the jungle, is in many respects tremendously appealing: he's a kind of Indian Huckleberry Finn, who has nothing but disdain for the clumsy humans in their crowded and smelly village. But while Mowgli's "brothers," the four wolf cubs, may accept him as their sibling and indeed their leader, Mowgli, unlike them, can never find a mate among the "Free People," and can never start a family such as the one that adopted him. From the very first story, Kipling is aware of this, and an undercurrent of melancholy is present in Mowgli's "freedom" throughout the tales.

Mowgli Today

The Jungle Book is at once a timeless work and a product of its own era: The appeal of Mowgli, the boy raised by wolves, is one that a child of any century can feel; but the values with which Kipling imbues the stories are very much of his own day (and were, in fact, rather old-fashioned even then). Readers of *The Jungle Book* today constantly have the strange

experience of being seduced by Kipling's story-telling power into identifying with Mowgli and his friends, and then bumping their shins when Kipling champions some sentiment that we recognize today as chauvinistic, even inhumane. (Kipling's politics were only beginning to fall out of date by the 1890s, but his brutality and occasional sadism were noticed by some critics even then.)

It is not surprising, then, that subsequent generations have taken from *The Jungle Book* those elements that still speak to them and altered (sometimes radically) the rest. The cartoon version of *The Jungle Book* tells a simple story of Mowgli living with his Jungle friends and trying to avoid being eaten by Shere Khan and Kaa (See previous page); the recent live-action film actually depicts British imperialism in an unfavorable light. The 1942 British version, an adventure film intended for adults, is the only film version to use one of Kipling's actual tales for its plots (it adapts a souped-up version of "The King's Ankus"). The Classics Illustrated adaptations of the three stories are faithful to their plots, but do not really address the stories' political overtones.

Although future generations will continue to take from *The Jungle Books* what they like and discard the rest, the stories as Kipling wrote them will always retain readers, whatever they may think of the tales' darker elements. Kipling's genius as a story-teller comes through in adaptations, but is best appreciated through his own vigorous and supple prose, which possesses the rare ability to reward children and adults alike.

Study Questions

•Mowgli is raised by wolves, but his best friends (and teachers) are a bear and a python—not pack animals at all. In what way does Mowgli behave like a pack animal, and in what way is he more like a lone hunter?

•Kipling's Jungle is in many ways an allegory of human society as Kipling felt it should be. Has Mowgli's childhood in the Jungle outfitted him for living in human society? Give examples.

•Is there a reason why Kipling makes Bagheera the panther a good figure and Shere Khan the tiger such a bad one?

•Aside from Mother Wolf, none of the animals in *The Jungle Book* is a female. Why?

•How would a twentieth century version of *The Jungle Book* differ from Kipling's? Give details and reasons.

•Imagine Mowgli's first year back among humans, after the end of the book. What would be the hardest things for him to learn? What would be most frightening to him?

About the Essayist:

Gregory Feeley is an encyclopedist, critic, and novelist, the author of *The Oxygen Barons* (Ace, 1990). His essays have appeared in *The Atlantic Monthly*, *The Washington Post*, and *New York Newsday*.